GW00865544

THE COWARDLY KNIGHT

The Cowardly Knight

by

DAMIAN WOODS

Copyright © D Woods 2020.
1st Edition
Published December 2020.

For my Parents

Prologue

THE HORSE GALLOPED FASTER, sensing the danger from above. The Knight could sense it too.

Above, the huge creature beat its wings, making the surrounding trees sway and creak, leaves flying like hail. It was coming round again, wheeling closer and closer.

The Knight urged his steed on, hooves pounding like thunder. The forest path was wide. Too wide. There was no cover. Ahead, he could see moonlight cutting through the trees.

Above, the winged beast came closer.

The Knight could feel its breath. Each exhale brought a cloud of hot fog, like steam, pouring over him like a blanket. The horse felt it too, and began to gallop yet faster. Ahead, the trees began to thicken. Cover at last, the Knight thought.

The dragon was almost on him now. The Knight could smell rotten meat.

Suddenly, the trees surrounded them like a wall. The creature roared in anger, breaking off its pursuit.

The Knight cheered but the horse could not slow down. The trees made it hard to see ahead. The horse's hooves still pounded on the forest floor.

Safety now, thought the Knight. The dragon will surely lose interest. He tried to slow his horse down. He pulled on the reins, but the poor steed was too frightened. He tried and tried but it was no good.

Then the trees were gone. And the floor gave way to nothing.

Suddenly, they were flying…

1

THE VOICE ON THE car radio announced the time as 1pm before introducing a song from way back when. Simon Phillips wasn't really listening. He had his eyes on the road. His eleven year old daughter, Alyssa (Ally for short) was sat in the back, literally boxed in tight by everything they owned in the world. She had barely enough room to fold her arms in disgust.

Simon had recently got a new job as Curator of Greymere Castle and all of the objects and exhibits on display there. Problem was, it was over 150 miles away from their old home. Which meant a big move. A move away from friends, from family and from the house he had lived in since before Ally was born.

Ally was not happy, hence the folded arms.

Simon (henceforth known as Dad) was blatantly unaware of his daughter's feelings. He thought he was helping. He was trying to help the both of them. Two years ago his wife, Ally's Mother, had died of cancer. The memories were still raw and painful. Neither of them had gotten to the point that they could leave the painful memories behind. Maybe this move would help, he thought. A fresh start. A new beginning. It wouldn't be easy.

He was sure it would help.

He was so completely unaware of his daughter's eyes burning into the back of his head.

Ally missed her Mum a great deal. Sometimes it hurt. She looked a lot like her Mum. Bright eyes, beautiful smile, strong, determined jaw.

Ally loved to run. Cross-Country. She was good at it and it helped her process her feelings about her Mum. She had no idea if there would be anywhere to run around near Greymere Castle.

She had been playing various games on her phone for the whole journey, angrily launching birds at pigs and destroying alien spaceships. Her phone battery had died about half an hour ago and she was in too much of a mood to ask her Dad to put it on charge up front. She had her Mum's temper. Dad was too passive at times, she thought.

And he was a nerd. He loved his job. Sifting through 'old-stuff'. Learning all about where this and that came from and what it was used for.

Problem was, Ally was a nerd too. She loved History and reading all about the same kinds of things her Dad loved. She would never tell him that though. Not right now. She was too mad at him for dragging her away from everything she knew. Including her Mum. She was still back there. Her memory. Her smell. It was in their old house and now they were leaving it behind.

"Nearly there, Honey," said Dad.

"Humumm," she replied.

She didn't feel like talking.

2

"THERE IT IS!"

The sound of her Dad's voice brought her out of her daydreaming haze.

The car had been trundling along for about another half-hour. The view outside the windows had become more rural, green hills and trees replacing villages and towns. There were still buildings of course, but much more spaced out. She shifted in her seat to look over his shoulder at the oncoming view. And indeed, there it was.

The tree line ahead had much more regular and angular shapes deposited in its middle. They were the battlements of Greymere castle, pushing upward into the sky. Ally couldn't help but be impressed.

"What do you think? It's pretty cool, huh?" Dad said excitedly.

"Yeah," she said, non-committedly.

"Just think, we're actually going to be living in the grounds!"

There was a cottage in the grounds of the castle that came with the job. Ally had seen pictures. It was the very definition of 'twee'. And she was going to be spending the weekend shifting boxes and bags into it, trying to somehow make it a home. And then came the new school. New teachers. New classes. New pupils. Dad, of course, had told her that she would 'make new friends in no time'. She thought she was happy enough with the ones she had.

Pulling into the grounds, Ally could see the huge castle sitting on top of a hill, almost as if the hill itself had been put there especially for it.

The main body of the castle was probably 13th Century, while certain, more solid additions had been added much later. There were signs pointing towards the Visitors Centre and the Gift Shop, as well as the Castle entrance itself. There was also another side-road which led to the cottage.

"Let's go see the cottage," said Dad, turning off.

As they moved around the road, Ally looked up at the huge structure, a dark silhouette surrounded by harsh daylight.

3

THE COTTAGE LOOKED MUCH like the pictures. Still twee, but a bit more ramshackle. Dad stopped the car outside and turned off the engine. He stepped out, stretching his limbs and his back. Ally did the same.

"Not bad, eh?" said Dad excitedly. He was trying so desperately to sound enthusiastic for Ally and even for himself. Problem is, Ally could sense it.

"Dad, you don't have to do this."

"Do what?"

"Sound so... excited about everything, ok?"

. He sighed. "I'm just, trying to make the best of things, alright?" There was some pleading in his voice. "It's like an adventure."

"It's not and adventure to me." Her voice suddenly got higher. This was an argument brewing.

Dad didn't like arguing. He was a talker. He turned toward her wanting to talk it out. Then suddenly, a rather grizzled old man stepped out of the cottage.

"You Simon Phelps?" shouted the man.

Dad turned away from Ally, keeping his eyes on her until the last moment.

"Phillips," he replied.

"Phillips," the man mumbled.

He sloped over to them. His face would be described as rugged. His cheeks were red and his eyes lidded. Ally thought he looked half-asleep.

"I'm Henry Sampson" said the old man. "I'm the Head Groundskeeper."

"Nice to meet you" said Dad. They shook hands.

"I was just checking the place over for you. Electric is on, so is the gas. Here."

He pulled the cottage keys out of his pocket and handed them over.

"Thank you."

"If you need me for anything, my number is on a pad next to the phone." He coughed slightly.

"Thank you," said Dad again. "I've got a meeting with the staff at nine on Monday morning. Will you be there?"

Henry nodded. "I'll be there. You get yourself settled. Get to know the place."

Henry looked at Ally. He nodded. "Young lady."

Ally wasn't really sure how to respond. She just gave a causal wave. "Uh, hi."

He turned back to the cottage, nodded, and then started to walk away, giving a brief wave as he went.

Dad turned toward Ally. It wasn't really the time to talk. She wasn't in the mood. He could see it. Maybe later, he thought.

"Come on" he said, deflated. "Let's take a look."

The inside of the cottage had a pleasant feel. It was busy, as in full. Every corner, every space seemed full of pictures, plaques, paintings, boxes and chests. Ally thought the cottage had become some kind of extra storage space, like it had the overspill of relics from the castle itself.

Dad was immediately captivated, looking at the bits and bobs. Ally moved through the space, seeing the tiny kitchen with its old, sturdy gas stove. The stairs were next to it. She walked up, each of the stairs creaking and croaking like bullfrogs as she went. There were some more steps, a little sturdier than a regular ladder, leading up to the attic.

She explored further. There was the bathroom, again a little small, but clean. Finally, the bedrooms. The master bedroom looked okay. It had two large wooden wardrobes in it. She moved on to what would be her own room. The door whined as she opened it. The sunlight streamed through the small window, cutting the room in half with a swathe of yellow.

Ally sat on the bed. She sank a little into the thick mattress. There was a bedside cabinet, a chest of drawers, a smaller wardrobe that looked related to the ones in the Master Bedroom.

Well, here we are, she thought. No turning back. Nothing I can do about it now.

I wonder if there's Wi-Fi?

4

The whole town was old. Old houses, old shops, old buildings.

The school was old, too.

Inside was a lot sunnier. The classes were cheerful and the teachers seemed nice.

The pupils weren't bad either. A number of them had said hello and introduced themselves. Ally had been pleasant in return but she didn't really feel like talking. She had spent the weekend with her Dad moving everything into the cottage. Once their possessions had found a place, Dad had announced 'cosy', which Ally thought was code for 'cramped'. The rest of the time was spent in almost silence, opportunities for conversation, like meal-times, passed in an awkward atmosphere.

It was dinner-time at school now. Ally had had her lunch and was in the library. She enjoyed the quiet. She sat in the corner at a table, head huddled in her arms. Thinking. She had so much to think about. She didn't want to fall out with her Dad but she wasn't ready to be all pleasant with him either. It was going to take time. And she'd probably get used to the move. And the school. But not yet. She couldn't allow everything to be alright just yet.

"Mind if I sit here?"

Ally looked up.

There was a boy standing there, bag on his shoulder. "Is that ok?"

"Sure," she said, sitting up.

He put his bag on the table and sat opposite her. "I'm Alex."

"Uh, hi. I'm Ally."

"Yeah, I know. We're in the same class." He smiled.

"We are? Sorry, I didn't really notice."

"I thought so. You looked a bit distracted."

He wore black-rimmed glasses that had slipped slightly down his nose. He pushed them back up. He had a pleasant manner and a nice smile. Ally couldn't help but smile back.

"I'm sorry about that," she said. "I've just moved here and, I've had some, well…" she started to flounder.

"It's okay" he said. "We've only just met. No need to tell me everything right now."

"How come you're not with your own friends?" she asked. Secretly glad he was right where he was.

"Uh, well, I kind of like the library, to be honest. Quiet in here. My mates like football and I'm not much of a player and they know that."

"That's nice, you know, that they know you like that. Good friends." She said it rather sadly, thinking of her own friends 150 miles away.

"I've got another reason," he said awkwardly.

"What's that?"

He started to look a bit red. His eyes looking toward the table.

"I wanted to meet you."

"Oh?" She couldn't help but smile. And her cheeks started to feel warm.

"Sorry," he said. "Is it too much? Am I weirding you out?"

"A bit," she laughed. "But it's okay."

5

THE REST OF THE school day had passed a lot more pleasantly for Ally. She and Alex had talked all the way through lunch-time. She felt comfortable with him. He was interested in books. He loved reading all kinds of stories – horror, science-fiction, fantasy. He had a good imagination. She opened up about her Mum. He seemed genuinely sorry. He was also fascinated by her Dad's job. He had never been inside the castle before. Oh sure, he'd been around it, but like a lot of people who live near famous landmarks, he had never actually been. His parents never had the time to take him. His Dad was a Dentist, Mum ran the local Café. Long hours that meant not much family-time. Holidays were good, but they were always in destinations reached by boat or plane.

For the first time since arriving, Ally was glad her Dad worked in the castle.

"Maybe I can get you in there, sometime?" she said, smiling.

"Awesome!" he replied.

When Dad picked her up at home-time, she waved at Alex through the window. He waved back.

"Did you have a nice day?" Dad asked, almost nervous.

"It was good," she said. "Better than I thought it was going to be."

He visibly relaxed. "I'm so glad. Have you made any friends?"

"One so far."

"Great. What's her name?"

"Uh, it's Alex. He's a boy." She looked out of the car window.

Her Father smiled. "A boy, huh? Quick work, kiddo."

Ally actually laughed. "Dad! He's just a friend."

"Sure he is," he teased.

She hit him playfully on the arm. They both laughed. He beamed. This was like old-times.

Ally decided to be pleasant with her Dad way ahead of schedule.

They actually talked with each-other at the dinner-table that night. Dad spoke a bit about his day. The staff seemed nice, he said. There were a lot of items to look after and sort. He would have plenty to do.

She went up to her room after dinner. There were still boxes unopened. She decided to put some stuff out. Opening the first box, she was met with a smile very similar to her own. It was a picture of her Mum.

She took it out of the box like it was a holy relic. Sitting back on her bed, she stared at the picture. She became lost in her Mum's eyes. Memories flooded back, good and bad. A teardrop fell on the picture.

Ally wasn't embarrassed by tears. She let them flow.

"Miss you, Mum."

Then she started to hear wailing. Loud, heaving sobs.

"Dad?"

Ally put the picture on her bed and stood up. She walked out of her room and went to the top of the stairs. It had started to get dark outside.

"Dad?" She shouted. "Are you okay?"

"Sure, honey," he shouted back. "Why?"

"Uh, nothing. Just checking." She looked about her, opening her ears, trying to find the source of the strange sound. Had she just imagined it?

Suddenly, she heard the wailing again. It was muffled. Muted somehow.

It was coming from above her.

She looked up at the entrance to the attic. She walked over to the foot of the steps.

The wailing stopped.

She put her foot on the first step.

"Ally!" Shouted her Dad from below.

She jumped.

"Start getting ready for bed, okay?" he said.

"Okay."

She moved away from the steps, wondering what on earth was up there. Could the wind have made a noise like that?

She would have to find out.

6

I̲T WAS FRIDAY LUNCH-TIME at school and Ally and Alex were sitting together in the yard. The sun was shining and the sound of other children talking and playing filled the air like tinkling glass.

Ally had considered telling Alex about the strange crying, but she was still questioning whether or not she really heard it. She tried to push it from her mind.

"So, how are you finding it here?" asked Alex. "Is it getting easier?"

"Yeah, I guess," she said.

"You don't sound too convinced." He adjusted his glasses.

"Well," she sighed, "some days are better than others. My Dad is so desperate for things to be good, you know?"

"But things are good! You've met me, haven't you?" said Alex, smiling.

Ally smiled back and nudged him with her shoulder.

"Listen, I haven't asked my Dad yet, but, would you like to see inside the castle?"

Alex's eyes brightened with interest. "Wow, really?"

"Yeah, why not? I've kind of got an insider."

"I'd love too, if it's with you. Uh…" Alex stumbled over his words, his cheeks flushing red. "I mean, if it's okay with you. And your Dad."

Ally couldn't help but smirk. "It'll be fine. I'll try and arrange something. But be prepared, he will want to know all about you."

"I'll try and make a good impression."

The sound of the school bell rang out. Alex was thankful for the distraction from his embarrassment. They both stood and began walking over to the building. Ally decided to chance her arm. She didn't want to mention the strange noises she heard in the attic, but maybe there was another angle.

"Do you know of any of the history around this place? The castle, the grounds, stuff like that?"

"Uh, not really. Well, nothing concrete anyway," he replied.

"What do you mean, nothing concrete?"

"There's local legends and stuff. As I say, I've never been in the castle, so I don't know *facts* or anything."

Her interest was piqued. "Local legends? What kind?"

"The best one is about a dragon that used to terrorise this place, like, hundreds of years ago."

"And Knights in shining armour to fight it off, right?" she said, smiling.

Alex suddenly stopped. "Actually, no. No one has ever mentioned a Knight. Weird. There usually is one."

"Yeah," she said. "Usually."

They both walked into school.

7

As Alyssa had gotten used to the village and the surrounding areas, she had started walking to and from school. She didn't mind when the weather was good.

She walked toward her cottage, waving at Henry Sampson as he trundled by on his sit-on lawnmower. He turned off the ignition and came to a stop next to her.

"Afternoon, young miss." he said in his patented growl.

"Hi Mr Sampson. You had a good day?" said Ally brightly.

"Always something to do," he replied, neither sounding good nor bad. "You all settled in?"

"Yeah. It's taken a while but I quite like it now."

He nodded slowly. "Cottage been treating you well?"

Ally wasn't quite sure what he meant, so she just said "Um, yeah. Very nice." Then a thought struck her. "Is that a surprise?"

"No, no" he replied quickly. "Just sometimes, you know, old houses, cottages and the like, they have their funny ways. Not to everyone's taste."

Alyssa was about to ask more, when Henry suddenly turned on the ignition and the lawnmower roared to life. "You take care now" he said, as he tumbled off slowly into the distance.

She waved after him, shrugged and walked into the cottage. Surprisingly, her Dad was already home. Must have been an early finish today, she thought. She peered into the living room and saw him on the couch, asleep. Placing her school bag on the floor by the door, she walked over to him. His left hand hung loosely at his side, his head lolled gently up and down, matching the slow rhythms of his breathing. His right hand rested on his chest, clutching a framed photograph.

Ally recognised it immediately.

It was a holiday picture of the whole family. Taken about 3 years ago, it was the last holiday they had experienced together. She looked at the photo and saw their smiling faces looking back. Mum, Dad and her. They were framed by a beautiful blue sky.

Heaven, she thought.

She looked at her Father again, sleeping peacefully. She smiled. Ally had thought so much about how Mums death had affected her and not much about how it had affected her Dad. He had always seemed so strong through it all. She realised then, he had remained strong for her.

Ally walked around the back of the couch, leant over and kissed his forehead. He stirred briefly then fell back into sleep.

She grabbed her school bag and walked quietly upstairs. Throwing her bag on the bed, she was about to open it when she heard the wailing sound again.

It was time to find out more about it.

Ally walked to the bottom of the rickety ladder leading to the attic. She took a determined breath and began walking up.

Ally reached the hatch to the attic. She pushed against it and it creaked open.

The wailing grew louder.

She stepped up into the attic.

It was as she expected it to be. A musty smell, a lot of old wooden and cardboard boxes smothered in dust, piled in the middle of the floor. There were old portraits and piles of mouldy books draped with cobwebs scattered about. Here and there, blades of yellow sunlight pierced the old roof, illuminating the gloom.

And still the wailing grew louder.

Ally crept around the pile of boxes, sensing the source of the sound was near.

She moved cautiously. Quietly. I really hope this is a good idea, she thought.

Too late now.

She peered around a particularly dusty wooden box. And there it was.

8

ACTUALLY, THERE *HE* WAS.

It was the figure of a man. He was sat on a box with his back facing her. The shoulders were shaking with each sob.

Ally was suddenly frozen with fear. A man? In the attic? How could they not know? Why was he there? What did he want? She was about to slowly creep away. She didn't want this stranger to know she was there. He could be dangerous. Or weird. Or both.

But then she noticed something about this man. In fact, she noticed a few. The first was the way he was dressed.

He was dressed in armour. Old fashioned armour. Like a Knight.

The next thing she noticed was the glow. He had a strange ethereal glow all about him. Was it the sunlight? No. This glow had a tinge of blue, not yellow.

Then the final thing. Maybe the most important of all.

She could see *through* him. He was like tracing paper. Dim shapes of other boxes and hanging pictures could be seen through his body.

Now children have much better imaginations than adults. Their minds are more open. Their willingness to believe in the impossible, the strange, the wonderful, so much freer. And so Ally knew, there and then, exactly what she was looking at.

It was a ghost.

And as amazing as that was, Ally was scared to the core. It was time to move.

She involuntarily sniffed and a plume of dust shot up her nose. Between the shock and panic, she sneezed.

The Knight stopped sobbing. He raised his head at the noise.

Ally ran.

She ran toward the attic hatchway, but in her urgency, she knocked it closed with her foot. It slammed with a thud.

She bent down, looking for a handle but not finding one. She looked up, and was suddenly face to face with the ghost Knight.

She screamed.

He screamed.

Ally shouted the only words that had marched to the forefront of her brain. "Don't hurt me!"

The Knight's head turned to the side like a curious dog. "Hurt you?" he said. "Why dear lady, why would I hurt you? In fact, I was going to ask that you not hurt me!"

Ally's panic began to subside. "What?" she said.

He chuckled. "Well, I know you can't actually hurt me," he said. "But I wanted to check that you were alright."

"Um, I don't know what's going on right now." She was confused. She was shaken. He was speaking. And he was polite!

"Why don't you sit down?" said the Knight, bowing courteously toward a box.

"Ooookay" she said. Ally sat on the box, never once taking her eyes from the ghostly figure.

"Did I scare thee?" he asked.

"Did you what?"

"Mmm? Oh, sorry. My words, they tend to lapse into old-fashioned talk. You'd think it wouldn't happen all that often now, given how long I've been hanging round this cottage. Lots of families. I've tried to pick up on the common parlance."

The casual way in which this phantom was having a conversation with her, kept Ally stunned to her seat. She watched him as he spoke. He seemed to be about thirty or so. With a straggly beard. He was smiling brightly but his eyes were deep and even a little melancholy. Well, she thought, he is a ghost after all. If you're dead, you're going to be a bit sad about it.

"What's your name?" she asked.

"How remiss of me!" He bowed low. "I am Hugo. Hugo Greymere. But you can call me Hugo."

"Hugo *Greymere*?!" said Ally excitedly. "You mean, that castle is yours?"

The Knight suddenly became a little evasive. "Indeed, um, yes. It's certainly, in the family." Ally was about to ask more when Hugo turned the conversation away. "And what, may I ask, is your name?"

"It's Ally. Alyssa."

"Allyalyssa? How unusual."

"No, no," she laughed. "My name is Alyssa, but people call me Ally for short."

"Ahhhhh" he said, nodding sagely. "And what would you prefer I call you?"

"Ally, is fine."

He bowed again. "A pleasure." He hesitated a moment. "Do you mind if I ask thee a question?"

"Of course."

"How did you come to find me up here?"

Ally was confused. Didn't he know how much noise he had made sobbing and wailing? "Um, I heard you, uh, crying."

Hugo was suddenly embarrassed. And amazed. "You *heard* me?"

"Yeah. Why? Hasn't anybody else ever heard you before?"

"Not to my knowledge. You are the first person I have spoken to since, since…" he trailed off.

Ally finished the sentence for him. "Since you died?"

Hugo walked away, lost in a memory. "Yes."

"I'm sorry," said Ally. "I didn't mean to upset you."

The Knight shook himself off. "Don't be silly. I've been dead a good while now. No use being upset about it, ay? Out of curiosity, what year is it?"

She told him.

He stumbled back and sat on another box. "Gracious. That long?"

He seemed to drift again.

"Can I ask you something?" she said finally.

"Of course," he said, brightening.

"How can I see you? And hear you? I mean, my Dad hasn't heard a single thing."

"Tis a good question. Many families have lived in this cottage and on this land over the years. Some, I feel, may have heard me. Many more have not. Out of those who have perceived me, most have been children. Maybe it is innocence?"

"Innocence?"

"Why yes," he said. "A child's mind is so much freer than an adult. An adult's mind is chained by experience."

She nodded. It was as good an explanation as any.

Ally thought she had better get going. Her Father must have slept through the commotion but she didn't want to have to answer awkward questions. How could she get him to believe there was ghostly Knight in the attic? Could she really believe it herself?

She looked back over at him and was surprised to see that he was looking at her.

"Tell me Ally, have you been touched by a sadness?"

How could he know, she thought?

Ally found herself answering without any hesitation at all. "Yes." She said. "My Mum. She died recently."

"I am very sorry," he said. "You know, grief is like a cloak. It hangs around you. It can be seen."

"Really?"

"Oh yes. But you mustn't let it drag you down."

Ally knew her Mother's death had hit her hard. She never felt she had been able to say a proper goodbye. She never realised it showed so much. I suppose, she thought, being a ghost, he could see it.

"I need to get going," she said.

Hugo's shoulders sagged. Ally saw.

"But I'll come back," she added.

Hugo smiled. "Really?"

"Of course!"

Hugo stood proudly. "I would like that very much."

Ally went back over to the attic hatchway. There was a thin block of wood nailed into it. She hadn't seen it before in all the panic. Grasping hold of it, she lifted the hatchway easily. She started to step down the ladder. About halfway down, she looked back at Hugo.

"Sorry I scared you" they both said together. Ally laughed, Hugo smiled.

"I look forward to seeing you again, Ally." For the final time that visit, Hugo bowed.

Ally was still smiling as she closed the hatchway behind her.

She washed her dusty hands in the bathroom, thoughts and questions swimming around her head. Why was he crying? Why is he haunting the cottage and not the castle? After all, the castle was his official home, wasn't it? Would anyone believe her? Would Alex? Before tackling these questions, she knew she had to find out more. Maybe a tour round the castle would help. She had promised Alex. And now, it was a fact-finding mission.

She walked back downstairs. Amazingly, her father was still sleeping. She was about to wake him when his eyes slowly opened. He smiled.

"Hey, kiddo."

"Hi Dad."

He yawned like a lion. "Must have dropped off."

He placed the holiday picture on the small table next to the couch. He casually looked at his watch. His eyes widened considerably.

"Look at the time! Oh, Ally I'm so sorry. You should have woke me up! What about tea?"

"Dad, it's okay. You obviously needed the rest." She sat next to him.

"I'm sorry" he said again. "What about pizza? Shall I order one?"

"That would be great," she said.

Dad began rummaging around for a takeaway menu.

"Uh Dad, I've got a favour to ask…"

9

THE VISIT TO THE castle happened the very next day. Alex's Mum had a shift at the Café and Dad had a golf session booked in. It was the only way to relax after a week of pulling teeth and gazing into the bottomless pit of people's mouths.

Ally and her father waited for Alex at the castle entrance. His Dad dropped him off on the way to the golf course, waving pleasantly as he drove away. Ally's Dad couldn't help but tease her as they were waiting.

"I wonder if he'll bring flowers?" he asked mischievously.

"Daaaaad" she replied, hitting him half-heartedly on the arm.

He laughed.

Alex approached them. "Hi Ally."

"Hi Alex. This is my Dad."

Alex suddenly became very formal. He held out his hand for Ally's Dad to shake. "Pleased to meet you, sir."

Dad shook his hand. "Pleased to meet you too, young man. Very polite."

He leaned into his daughter with a playful look in his eye. "This one's a keeper" he whispered.

"Daaad" she said again, quietly and through gritted teeth.

"So," Dad said, ignoring her completely, "you've got two options here. Option one, you can wander around the castle by yourselves. Option two, I can be your very own personal tour guide."

Ally could feel the prickles of fear rising up her spine. "One" she said, a bit too quickly. "Option one."

"Very well," he said, feigning disappointment. "I'll leave you to it. Come find me about 12 and I'll sort you some dinner. Have fun!"

He winked at Ally and walked away toward his office.

"Sorry about him," said Ally.

"It's okay," laughed Alex. "That's parents, right?"

They walked into the castle.

Ally couldn't deny it, she was as fascinated by the artefacts and surroundings as Alex was. Tapestries, suits of armour, weapons. As old as they were, the metal glinted in the dim light, as if newly forged. "This is so cool," said Alex. "I should have come here a lot sooner."

Ally looked closely at the armour. It looked very similar to the armour Hugo had been wearing. Family heirlooms, she thought. She continued to look about for any evidence, for any clue, that would give her more information about Hugo Greymere.

They stepped into the next room. This could be where the answers lay. The walls had been decorated with the family crest. There were also paintings and tapestries of Knights in battle and on horseback. One picture even showed a Knight facing off against a hideous dragon. Alex pointed at it.

"Must be what the local legend is based on," he said, adjusting his glasses. He walked over to take a closer look at it.

Ally was drawn to a large glass case, about the size of a dining table. Inside were some very old documents, brown and cracked with age, along with a large, thickly bound book, opened in the middle. The writing was, of course, extremely old-fashioned and hard to read. But some of the art work inside was beautifully done – burnished gold and royal blue.

What was incredibly clear though, was the information on display. It was a Greymere family tree. And a list of honours bestowed upon the family. Lots of Lords and Sirs. As well as some more elaborate titles. Lord Arthur Greymere, Protector of the Realm. Sir Francis Greymere, Slayer of Vikings and on it went. Nothing about a Hugo Greymere though.

Ally kept searching. Then she came to a part of the Family Tree that looked altered in some way. A name that had been crossed out. Erased.

She turned her attention to the book. There was something odd about it. Was there a page folded? No. Not folded.

Ripped.

There was a jagged edge all the way up the middle that jutted out near the top, as if someone had ripped it out from the bottom of the book and it veered off. She looked closer. There were words on it. Faded but readable.

'Sir Hu'

That's all that was there. The rip went straight past the 'u', cutting off the rest of the word. It had to be Hugo. His entry in the book had been purposefully removed.

But why was it ripped out? And was it his name that had been erased on the Greymere Family Tree? And would Hugo tell her about it?

"What are you looking at?" inquired Alex. He had walked over to her and was peering into the glass case.

"It's the Family Tree of the castle. All the Greymere's. Well, nearly all of them. Can you see there? A name has been scratched out." She pointed at it.

"Yeah. Cool. It's like a mystery. Wonder if we could solve it?" asked Alex excitedly. "Is there anyone we can ask?"

Ally was on the verge of blurting out everything there and then. "Maybe," was all she said.

After another hour of looking round, Ally's Dad fixed them up with some sandwiches. Ally asked if they could eat them at the cottage. Dad agreed. "Just don't make a mess."

10

ALLY BRUSHED THE SANDWICH crumbs off the kitchen table while Alex swilled out two empty glasses of orange juice. They had talked a lot about the cool stuff they had seen.

"Thanks so much for inviting me today. I've loved it," said Alex. "The castle was great and you know... spending time with you. I feel like I know you really well."

"Me too."

They gazed at each-other.

Alex felt like his face was suddenly on fire. "Kinda hot in here, right?"

Ally tried to help him change the subject. "Do you believe in ghosts?"

"Ghosts? I haven't really thought about it." He adjusted his glasses. "Why?"

Ally decided to tell him everything.

"Listen, I'm going to show you something. It's a bit weird and I don't know how you're going to take it."

Alex laughed a little nervously. "Wow. Should I be worried?"

"I don't know," said Ally flatly.

Now he was worried.

The attic hatchway creaked open. Ally stepped up into the attic and Alex followed. His eyes fell upon all of the boxes and old items scattered around the cramped space.

"Do you have any idea how much I would love to live in a place like this?" said Alex. Once again his enthusiasm for anything old and interesting had taken over.

"Keep that in mind" Ally replied with a smirk. She turned and spoke into the air. "Hugo! Hugo, are you here?"

Alex looked at her strangely. Who was Hugo? A pet rat?

Suddenly, almost casually, the luminous figure of Hugo Greymere passed through the wooden boxes and stood before both children. He smiled. "Greetings," he said.

Alex fainted.

A few minutes passed and Alex opened his eyes. He was looking up at the ceiling with Ally's face hanging over him. She was full of concern.

"Alex? Alex! Are you okay?"

"Yeah, I'm fine. I think. Was I dreaming?"

Ally took his arm and helped him up. As he sat up, he saw the ghostly form of the Knight sitting on a box, studying him. "Are you alright, young Sir?"

Alex scrambled across the floor backward into a corner. He bumped into boxes and curtains of cobwebs fell into his hair. "Is that uh, is he uh...?"

"A ghost?" declared Hugo, almost cheerfully. "A ghost I am. Don't worry, young man. I won't hurt you."

"He won't" pleaded Ally. "Let me explain."

Alex got up and dusted himself off, wiping grit from his spectacles while Ally filled him in on the story so far. By the time she got to the end, the three of them were sat around together in a circle.

"I'm guessing your Dad doesn't know about him?" asked Alex.

"No. You're the only one I've told."

Alex's cheeks flushed red a little.

Ally turned to Hugo. "We've been in the castle today."

"Oh?" said Hugo.

"It was amazing. All the armour and the swords and the paintings…"

"Yes, yes," flustered Hugo. "It's very nice."

"Why don't you want to talk about it?" asked Ally.

"Well it's… it's…," stammered Hugo. "It's private."

Alex leaned forward. "Um, Hugo, I hope you don't mind me saying this, but you're dead, right? What exactly are you so worried about?"

Hugo looked at them both. "It's a matter of honour."

"I'm sorry, Hugo. We didn't mean to upset you," said Ally softly. She didn't like seeing this rather proud ghost upset.

Hugo thawed. "You are forgiven. You must understand, there are some things that I find hard to discuss. Some things that a Knight should be able to deal with himself."

"But you don't have to now," said Ally. "You've never had friends before. You've got friends now."

"Friends?"

"Yeah" said Alex.

"You are both very kind. Tell me, what did you see in the castle that makes you so interested?"

Ally explained about the pictures. About the Family Tree. And about the book. She saw his shoulders slump with each new piece of information. He was quiet and still for many minutes.

"So," he said finally, "they have erased me."

"Who are 'they'?" asked Alex.

"My family of course" replied Hugo. "The Greymere's." The Knight stood, taking a few steps into the shadows. He glowed like a dim bulb in the dark.

"Honour is very important in my family. My father, grandfather, my brothers, all warriors. All heroes. I disgraced them. I disgraced myself."

Ally recalled the flowery titles and achievements listed in the Greymere Family Tree. A lot to live up to.

"I had a challenge," he said. "I failed. As such, I'm not allowed in the family home. Even as a ghost."

Ally stood and walked over to Hugo. "Can we help you in any way?"

"No," said Hugo sadly. "There is no help for me."

11

BOTH CHILDREN FELT BAD having to leave Hugo that way. He had brightened a little and said a hearty goodbye but they could see a deepening sadness in his eyes.

Alex's Dad was on his way. They both stood in the cottage living room, looking out of the window, waiting for the car to pull-up. "You know," he said, "I think that might have been the best day of my life."

"Don't be silly," said Ally, quietly thrilled.

"Of course it was! Castles? Ghosts? How can it get any better?"

"I kind of sprung him on you though, didn't I? I was really scared you hit your head."

"Nah," exclaimed Alex, brushing off his earlier embarrassment. "I'm fine. I really want to help Hugo, though. Somehow."

"Me too. There's got to be more information. I don't really want to ask him anymore. He was so upset."

Alex nodded in agreement. "Hold on," he said brightly, "we could look in the school library. There's a huge section on local history. Myths and Legends as well."

"Great. We'll have a look on Monday. I'd love to be able to tell Hugo we can help him."

"I'm thinking though," Alex murmured seriously. "You know that local legend about the dragon round here? You don't think that's mixed in with this somehow, do you?"

"A dragon?" she said, incredulously. "Dragons aren't real."

"I didn't think ghosts were real, either."

"Point," said Ally, nodding.

Just then, they saw Alex's Dad approaching in his car. "Well, here he is," he said, disappointment in every syllable. He turned to Alyssa.

"Hey Ally?"

"Yeah?"

Moving like lightning, Alex quickly kissed Ally on the cheek, shouting "See you Monday!" as he ran out of the house and into his Dads car.

She raised her hand and touched her cheek. "See you Monday," she said, to no one in particular. And smiled.

12

Monday morning couldn't arrive quickly enough.

Ally and Alex met at the school gates. Nervousness quickly gave way to smiles and they held hands across the yard, promising to meet in the library at lunch-time. When Alex arrived there, Ally already had a pile of books on the table.

"Found anything yet?" he asked, sitting opposite her.

"Not yet. Try this one." She passed an old, thick dusty book over to him.

Alex opened it and started flicking through. "Did you talk to Hugo again yesterday?"

"No. I thought I should just leave him be a little while."

"I still can't stop thinking about Saturday. It was just an amazing day."

Ally looked up at him. "Yeah. I was really worried about telling you. I thought you might think I was crazy."

"Oh, I know that much," he replied with a laugh.

For the next half-hour all you could hear were flicking pages and book covers slapping on table tops. They were both becoming restless and annoyed at not finding the answers they craved. Lunch-time was nearly over when Alex found a short story based, so the author said, on a local legend. The legend of a fearsome dragon and a cowardly knight.

"Ally! Look at this!"

She stood up and walked around the table. "What is it?"

She looked over his shoulder at the book, the two of them studying the story together. For the next 10 minutes, they both read about a small village, terrorised by a ferocious dragon. There was an illustration of a great, green scaly beast, with a terrifying wingspan. Its head was pointed towards the sky, with an inferno of flames spewing from its mouth.

The story told of a Knight who had promised to help rid the village of the great evil. He went into battle on his trusty steed, but the dragon was too strong. Its ferocity was too great, and so the Knight fled in terror, pursued by the beast.

The story ended with the Knight disappearing into the wilderness, eventually dying of shame. He was meant to have come from a great, courageous family of warriors. But with the cowardice of the Knight threatening to overshadow the family name, he was removed from all records, never to be heard from again.

Alex and Ally looked at each-other.

"Too much of a coincidence not to be true, don't you think?" said Ally.

"Definitely. But how can we help him out of it? How do we make him part of his own family again?"

"I don't know. Ghosts are supposed to exist because they have unfinished business, right? I mean, this sounds like some pretty serious unfinished business. I don't know how we get him out of it. But we will. I'm going to talk to him again tonight."

13

IT WAS AFTER 4PM when Ally walked into the cottage.

Dad tumbled straight out of the kitchen, very flustered. "Ally! I'm glad you're home. Look, I've got to go back into work."

She could see her father was in a whirl. "Dad! Calm down. What's wrong?"

"We had a school trip in today. Not local. Two of the children were, shall we say, a bit boisterous and they knocked over a suit of armour."

Ally was genuinely shocked. She imagined the noise all that metal made hitting the ground. "Is it okay?"

"Oh yeah, it's armour. It's not broken. But it's in pieces and I need to put it back together. Look, I'll just fix you some food and…."

He was pacing back and forth, just about to re-enter the kitchen when his daughter interrupted him.

"Dad. Stop!"

He stopped, looking right at her as if for the first time. "Huh?"

She walked over to him and put her hand on his arm.

"Dad, it's okay. I can fix something for myself. I'm a big girl now, you know?"

He looked at her and smiled, a little sadly perhaps. He put his fingers through her hair. "Yeah. You are, aren't you? Growing up. Too fast for my liking."

They hugged. It was as if Ally had found a dial and turned her Dad down from manic to calm.

"Now get going," she said.

"Okay, I'm going!" he said. He put his jacket on and headed out the door. "And don't forget to eat!" he called back.

But before she ate anything, Ally headed up to the attic. She climbed the creaky stairs and opened the hatchway. She heard no sobbing this time. No wailing. This time, she heard a fight.

"Have at thee!" shouted Hugo from behind the boxes.

She could hear the swiping noise of his sword, flying through the air. He was grunting and shouting.

She peered around the corner and saw Hugo in the throes of battle with an invisible foe. The space around him may have been cramped but as a ghost, his sword flew through walls and boxes, leaves a smoky ectoplasmic trail.

"Die, you beast!" he shouted.

He thrust the sword upward, into some huge colossus.

"Hugo?" she said.

The Knight gave an involuntary yelp. He almost toppled over.

"Ally!" he said breathlessly. I didn't see you there."

"Obviously," she replied, wryly. She sat on one of the boxes.

Hugo sheathed his sword. It may have been a spectral projection, but the metallic 'ring' it made when he slipped it back in the scabbard sounded very solid indeed. "What brings you here today?" he asked, sitting down opposite her. "Though I am very happy to see you."

"Listen Hugo," she began, in her best Dad-you need to listen to me-voice, "I need to tell you some stuff. And I need you to tell me some stuff as well. And you need to be honest."

"I feel like I am being scolded by my Mother."

"Alex and I have been doing some research."

"Oh?" he said, his eyebrows raised.

"It involves a Knight."

"Mmmmmmm"

"And a village. And a dragon."

"Ah," he exhaled, sadly. "You have heard the whole story, then?"

"Well, I don't know about the whole story. Most of it, maybe."

"I suppose now, you look at me, and you see a coward." He dropped his head, not able to look at her.

"No! Not at all. Hugo, you're my friend."

He looked back up at her. "Really?"

"Of course. Look, Alex and I, we want to help you."

He shook his head. "Like I said before, there is no helping me. Not against a dragon."

"Then the dragon was… real?" She almost spluttered the word.

He looked her directly in the eye. "As real as real can be."

"Well, you know, we don't really have dragons around right now."

"I know that!" declared Hugo. "They are extinct, thank goodness. Dragons, they are evil, vile creatures. Flying furnaces. They could bring entire villages to ruin. The fire inside them must always be ablaze. When it dies, the dragon cools and crumbles. If you were able to stab it in battle – actually pierce that scaly skin, the dragon would literally pop!"

"Is that what happened to you?" Ally asked quietly.

"What did the story say?" he asked.

"Well, uh, it said you wandered into the wilderness and died of shame."

"True, in some respects, I suppose." He sighed. "I did go into the wilderness. I fled there on my horse, away from the awful beast that was chasing me. I was meant to save a village. I was meant to join my family as a hero. Instead, I….." he suddenly began to mumble. "I….. meh hoff uh hiff."

"What?"

Hugo shuffled on the box, turning his face away. "I feh off uh hliff."

"Hugo!" exclaimed Ally loudly. "Just tell me!"

"I fell off a cliff."

Despite everything, Ally couldn't help but laugh. "You fell off a cliff?" she said, trying desperately to hold in her giggles.

Hugo looked at her. His straight face only made it worse. "Yes" he said calmly. "I fell off a cliff."

Ally could hold it in no longer. She laughed. "Sorry," she said, covering her mouth.

Hugo's face started to change. Slowly at first, but a smile began to form. His shoulders began to shake, until he too was laughing. "It is funny, I suppose. Ridiculous, really. Running away from one danger and literally face first into another!"

They laughed together for another few minutes. When eventually they both calmed down, Ally asked again. "So, is there anything that can be done?"

"There is something. A challenge. But the challenge is mine alone. Every 100 years, since my death, the battle is fought over again. That huge beast is brought back from whatever hell it now resides. And we fight. If I were to win, I would join my family. A true Greymere. But, in all honesty Ally, I am too afraid. A ghost I may be, but my fear is real."

"Have you ever tried to fight it?"

"I tried. My first 2 times, I tried. But I ran." He bowed his head. "I ran."

"You've got to try again, Hugo. You have to. You're not happy. You're lonely."

He stood, looking out at some invisible horizon. "The battle is even now closing in on me. Only a few days away. And I know I will lose yet again."

"That doesn't matter," said Ally. "As long as you fight with honour. Surely that's more important than winning. You know, my Mum lost her battle, too."

Hugo looked up at Ally.

"She was ill. So ill. But she fought. She fought it every day." Without realising, tears had begun to fall from her eyes. "She was the bravest person I ever knew."

"You are very brave too, Ally. I think you must have your Mothers courage."

Ally felt the tears on her face. She wiped them away.

"Maybe," he continued, "you could pass some of that courage onto me?"

She smiled at him. "Do you mean it?"

"Maybe it's time," he said.

14

BETWEEN HUGO, ALLY AND Alex, they determined that midnight the coming Saturday was the next anniversary of the Knight's battle with the deadly dragon. On that night, Hugo told them, he would materialize in the vast grounds of Greymere castle. The only night he was ever able to leave the cottage. Along with his horse, who he had named Blue, he would ride out to meet the threat. The dragon would follow soon after.

It was always the same, so his story went. The dragon would circle and swoop, breathing white-hot fire. He and Blue would try and find cover, to no avail. The trouble, he said, was trying to get the hulking brute to land. In the air, it was impossible. The fire would eventually consume them.

Dawn the following day, he would re-appear in the cottage and the long, lonely wait would begin again.

Friday's lessons couldn't be over quick enough. Ally and Alex both felt like they were wading through tar. The lunch-time library routine took place as usual.

"I'm going to sneak out of my house about eleven o'clock," said Alex, conspiratorially.

"What?" exclaimed Ally. "You can't do that. What if you get caught? What if something happens to you?"

"You can't tell me," Explained Alex calmly, "that you won't be doing the exact same thing. You know you'll be out there with him. Right in the thick of everything."

"But that's my choice," she said.

"And this is mine," he replied.

That night, while her father snoozed through a repeat of Midsomer Murders, Ally crept up into the attic. Hugo was waiting, sitting on his usual box.

"I've been waiting for you" he said, seriously.

"I can see that," said Ally, sitting opposite him. She could see concern in his eyes. "Are you nervous?"

"Oh, so nervous. More than I can really say. You know, this is the first time in centuries that I'm actually fighting to win."

"And do you think you will? Win?"

Hugo contemplated a while. She could see in his eyes, his mind working on an answer. "I do not know," he said finally. "What I do know is this, everything that you have said to me has helped me realise that winning is not always the answer." He stood. "For so long, I believed that only victory was enough to see me reunited with my family. Now I know that how you fight is as important as the winning or losing."

Ally smiled. "Glad to hear it."

He turned to her, a solemn look on his face. "To that end, I must ask both you and Alex not to help me."

Ally shot to her feet. "Why?!"

"It could be dangerous."

"But this dragon," pleaded Ally, "It's a ghost like you, right? It can't hurt me."

Hugo sighed heavily. "You believe in me, Ally. You and Alex. Because of that, you can see me. Hear me.

Who is to say that I could not harm you if I wanted? And if I can, maybe it can."

"But Hugo…"

He held up his hand to stop her mid-sentence. "No, Ally. I cannot risk it. You mean too much to me. Tomorrow night, I fight on my own."

Though she didn't say it, Ally had no intention of listening to him.

15

SATURDAY WAS AS PLEASANT as Ally could make it. Her father took her out for dinner. They walked around the pleasant little town and talked about their lives since moving there. Ally had no bad feeling toward her father any more. Those feelings had disappeared like smoke in the wind. Growing up was hard. So was loss. So was realising that the best thing to do isn't always the easiest. And the hardest route was sometimes the most rewarding.

Tonight, all of those lessons would come to fruition.

"Do you know how proud of you I am?" said Dad as they walked side by side, slowly heading home.

"Proud? Why?" she asked.

"Why? Your Mother's death was so hard. For both of us. Especially for you. I made a lot of decisions, including the one that brought us here. I just thought they were all for the best. I never really thought about what you wanted."

"I'm not going to lie, Dad. It was hard. I sort of hated you for a while."

He nodded. "I know. You don't hate me anymore though, do you, kiddo?"

He stopped in his tracks and turned toward her. She hugged him tighter than ever. He wrapped his arms around her, smiling from his very core.

"Love you, Dad."

That night, her father slept soundly. A sleep of contentment.

Hugo and Ally's farewell was strained and awkward. Ally knew she would be disobeying Hugo and Hugo couldn't help but be filled with doubt. He hoped his courage would be enough for the fight ahead, but there was nothing he could do to be sure.

"I won't say goodbye," he said. "I will say only, thank you. For everything."

It was 11.30pm when Ally left him and snuck outside in the grounds.

"Alex?" she whispered into the night.

No response.

She thought his parents must have caught him. She would rather that than have something bad happen to him on the way to the cottage.

There was a quiet rustling.

"Ally?" came his voice.

They met in the shadows. He could see her smile, even in the dark.

"I'm so glad you made it," she said.

"I'm just glad it isn't raining," he laughed.

Ally filled him in on all of Hugo's misgivings.

"Funny enough," Alex said "the same thing occurred to me. So, look…"

He reached into the backpack he had brought and lifted out a handful of fireworks. "Distraction" he said, simply.

"Where did you get those?"

"My Dad has them hidden in the garage. He has these big parties in the summer. He always likes to have fireworks."

"Wow," Ally said, impressed. "If your Dad finds out you've taken them you'll get..."

"Grounded," he finished. He shrugged. "Worth it."

Alex checked his watch. He pressed a button and the numbers lit up in the gloom.

It said 11:59.

With a quiet beep, the digits turned to 12:00.

Midnight.

The children searched their surroundings, not sure which direction to look. Then they saw a vague, glowing mist creep along the grassy expanse around them. It seemed to pulse somehow. Almost hum with a supernatural energy.

Then, Hugo began to materialize about thirty feet away. His image seemed to appear like a developing photograph. And next to him, his horse, Blue. They could see Hugo pat the horse, and speak to it in muffled tones they couldn't hear. They horse neighed with pleasure at seeing his master again. Hugo mounted the horse, the sound of clanking metal armour approaching them on the breeze.

"Where do you think the dragon will come from?" asked Alex.

Before Ally could answer, they heard a long, low growl. A deep, thrumming rumble that vibrated through the ground they knelt on.

In the distance, some way from Hugo, the mist seemed to pulsate.

There was something under it.

Something big.

Out of the smoke, peered a huge, horned head. It seemed to glow green. Sharp, knife-like teeth protruded from its partly opened mouth. The dragon's eyes were red, glowing with evil-intent. The scaly monster continued to emerge from the mist. A hulking, lizard-like body slunk out onto the ground, the tale sweeping around behind it with a *whoosh*.

When the body was fully in view, it stretched its massive wings like a child newly waking. They seemed to glisten and shine like the surface of the moon.

The dragon looked ahead and saw Hugo, fixating on him like a dog with its favourite toy.

Hugo drew his sword. The horse snorted.

Then the dragon roared, filling the sky with a sound like tearing metal.

"Still glad you came?" said Ally to Alex. Her eyes were wide with fear and wonder.

"Wouldn't miss it," replied Alex nervously, his face much the same.x

She took his hand.

"Let's help our friend."

Ahead of them, the dragon took to the sky.

16

THE DRAGON PUSHED ITSELF off the ground with a massive flap of its huge wings. A shockwave of air spread across the ground like a blanket. Ally and Alex almost toppled over. Alex looked back to see the spectral monster enter the air, lumbering at first, becoming more graceful. His eyes widened with amazement.

"Look at that!" he exclaimed.

Ally looked back and saw the dragon circling like a shark. Hugo wheeled his horse around and began to gallop around the expanse of the grounds.

"Where are we going to set up the fireworks?" she asked.

Alex looked around, settling on a spot. He pointed. "There."

They ran. Alyssa could feel her old Cross-Country muscles waking to the challenge.

The Knight halted his horse. The dragon had disappeared.

Hugo looked up. "Where are you, you wretch?"

Above, a blue-white speck circled.

"There you are."

The speck drew closer. The dragon was heading toward the ground like a spear. It opened its mouth.

"Oh dear," said Hugo. He flicked the reins and the horse bolted. The dragon came lower. Without warning, a column of flame shot from its gaping mouth. Hugo steered right as the flame passed by. While this ghostly inferno left the ground unmarked, the Knight felt the heat warm the metal of his armour. Inside it, he began to sweat.

The beast swooped around, coming in for a second pass. It began to dip down.

"Alright, Blue," Hugo said breathlessly. "Now's our chance."

As the dragon flew toward Hugo, the Knight galloped toward it. It came lower and lower, the air from the great animals flight sending ripples throughout the grass. Hugo could see it inhaling, the great chest filling out.

Then the flames came again.

Hugo banked right and the fire shot past. He raised his sword and struck the dragon in its huge underbelly. It screamed in pain and anger, taking to the sky again. The Knight cheered.

"I got him!" he shouted. "I actually got him." He laughed joyfully, forgetting for the moment that the dragon would be coming back.

He heard it roar.

Hugo looked. The beast was coming directly at him. He turned his horse back toward it, hoping to try the same move again. They lined up with each-other, like knights in a jousting tournament. Hugo and Blue began to charge forward. The dragon once again came close to the ground. Its mouth opened. Hugo readied his sword.

Then the dragon suddenly banked upward, whipping its huge tail toward the Knight with a great *snap!* It hit Hugo and Blue like a wrecking ball, sending them flying through the air. Blue tumbled to the ground with a grunt. Hugo landed almost ten feet away, the air completely knocked out of him.

The dragon landed with a thud that echoed into the cavernous night.

Hugo struggled up onto his elbows. His chest armour was dented. He looked over to Blue. His horse wasn't moving. He felt a great stab of loss. Looking over at the dragon, seeing it coming slowly toward him, he now knew this could never happen again. This was going to be the last time. The dragon may burn him to a cinder, it may take him into its vice-like jaws and crush him, but he would not passively go into the darkness of eternity. Never mind being a hero.

This was about honour.

He picked up his sword and painfully got to his feet. He stood as straight as his broken body would allow.

In his mind, the dragon was smiling. Taunting him. Its slimy tongue peeking out of its mouth.

Hugo brandished his sword, no longer the Cowardly Knight.

The dragon was only a few feet away.

This was it. Death had come for him.

Above, a firework exploded.

Hugo blinked in surprise and confusion. He looked up at the showering of twinkling stars falling down, fading as they reached the ground.

The dragon cocked its head. The noise was nothing like it had ever heard or seen before. There was another sharp hiss as a second firework took off into the sky. Hugo turned, looking for the source. He saw Ally and Alex grouped together on a slope that led up to the side of Greymere castle. In his heart, he felt a rush of joy at seeing them both. And then panic. They were in danger.

The second firework exploded. The dragon roared, sweeping its head back and forth, looking for the origin of its annoyance. And then finding it.

Hugo temporarily forgotten, the dragon began to move toward the children.

"Run!" shouted the Knight. "Run now!"

The dragon swept past him, knocking him to the ground again with a casual flick of its tail. He could only look on as it furiously sped toward his young friends.

"It's coming over here!" shouted Alex, quite unnecessarily.

Ally could see Hugo on the ground, helpless. She turned toward the dragon, its nightmare face looming out of the gloom toward her. She didn't know what to do. She could hear the pounding of its great clawed feet moving towards them. She could hear Alex shouting, begging her to run.

You believe in me, Hugo had said. Because of that you can see me and hear me. Who is to say that I could not harm you if I wanted? And if I can, maybe it can.

Maybe we can, thought Ally.

She turned toward Alex. "Shoot a firework at it!" she shouted.

She could see a question in his eyes, but he didn't ask it. He had a box of matches, again removed from his Dads garage. He struck one on the box and it flamed to life. Lighting the fuse of a firework, they both held it out in front of them, pointing it directly at the dragon. They turned their faces away, shielding their eyes from the bright flash as it launched, flying directly toward the great lizard.

The firework exploded in its face, covering its head in multi-coloured stars. The dragon roared in pain, fanning its great wings in frustration.

Alex saw their chance. He grabbed Ally's hand. "Come on!"

He pulled her way. They scrambled down the slope and started running, trying to get anywhere safe.

The dragon shook its head like an angry bear. It turned left and right, searching for its new enemies. Then it saw them. With an indignant snort, it began to pursue.

No matter how fast the children tried to run, each of the dragons strides brought it closer to them in no time at all. Running faster still, Ally and Alex stumbled to the floor in a tumble of limbs.

There was nowhere else for them to go. The dragon was upon them.

It reared its head back, the chest puffing out, preparing to fry them both with a final blast of fire.

Ally and Alex looked at each-other. No words could describe this moment. This was the end. They closed their eyes.

Suddenly, there was a great battle roar. A scream of ferocious power.

The children opened their eyes and saw…

Hugo.

He had crawled beneath the great beast. His left arm hung uselessly at his side, but with all the power he could muster, he thrust his right arm upward, plunging the sword he was holding deep into the dragon's chest.

The beast seemed to inhale slowly and the chest expanded like a balloon.

Hugo pulled the sword out sharply, the effort sending him sprawling to the ground.

The dragon reared up, stretching its great wings. And with a final roar, the dragon exploded in a cloud of ash, falling like rain to the ground. As it landed, it disappeared like melting snow.

Ally and Alex let out breaths they didn't realise they were holding. They looked over at Hugo.

He wasn't moving.

17

They scrambled quickly over to the fallen Knight.

He was lying still, with his eyes open, gazing up at the sky.

"Hugo?" said Ally, her voice quivering. "Hugo? You did it. You got him."

Hugo blinked.

Alex and Ally smiled.

"You're okay!"

Hugo looked around him as if newly seeing.

"How do you feel?" asked Alex.

The Knight couldn't help but laugh. He looked at them both with a smile. "Alive."

"What happens now?"

"I don't know," said Hugo, groaning as he got to his feet. "I've never got this far before."

They looked about them. All was quiet and still. The ethereal mist had gone. Then Ally saw something. "Look!" she pointed. They turned.

A Knight was standing about twenty feet away from them. A ghost, like Hugo, but resplendent in a scarlet cloak. Its armour gleaming.

Hugo whispered one word. "Father."

Lord Greymere drew his sword, the scarlet cloak

flowing on a spectral breeze. With a sweeping motion, the Knight stabbed the blade into the ground. A white circular wave swept outward over the landscape – over Blue's lifeless body, over the children, over Hugo. An intense white light filled their eyes. When it faded, Hugo stood straight, his armour repaired, a scarlet sash now draped over his shoulder.

There was a grunt. They looked and were overjoyed to see Blue, alive and proud again, trotting over to them. The horse nuzzled Hugo happily. In the distance, the imperious Knight waited patiently.

"This is it then," said Hugo.

"You've earned this," Ally said, holding back tears.

"I couldn't have done it without you." Hugo looked at her. Tears welled in his eyes. "Both of you."

"I'm going to miss you," Ally said, her tears finally breaking like waves on the shore.

Hugo embraced her. He felt solid in her arms. "Your mother would be so proud of you. You have her strength, her spirit."

Ally held him tighter. After another moment, she let him go and stepped back.

Hugo shook Alex's hand. "Take care of each-other."

The Knight smiled at them. He turned reluctantly away from them both. Taking the reins of his horse, he walked towards Lord Greymere, Blue clopping beside him. Ally and Alex stood like statues, watching him go. They saw Hugo approach, kneeling before his father.

Lord Greymere pulled the sword from the ground. Hugo bowed his head. Lord Greymere tapped the sword on Hugo's left shoulder with a 'ting' of metal on metal. He lifted the sword over Hugo's head and tapped his right shoulder, knighting him finally as part of the family of warriors. With that final 'ting', white light shone once more, blazing like a fire. Then in a moment, it was gone.

Hugo, Blue and Lord Greymere had disappeared.

The children cried openly, then embraced each-other tightly.

It was over.

18

THE NIGHT'S EXCITEMENT HAD neither been noticed nor commented upon.

Alex had made it home safely, but planned to return the following day.

At the breakfast table, Ally's father could sense something was amiss. Not wrong, but different. It seemed she had been crying.

"Thinking about Mum?" he asked gently, unsure of what else to say.

"I feel," she said, "like I've finally said goodbye."

He walked over to her. She stood up and they hugged.

The castle was open to visitors on a Sunday, but for less hours.

Alex and Ally walked through the cool stone corridors, holding hands. They made their way to the room holding the Greymere Family Tree. They both felt that something would be different but they weren't sure what. Maybe nothing, they thought. Maybe it's just a feeling.

They walked over to the glass case. Ally searched for the place that had been altered. Blank. It wasn't blank anymore. There it was written-

Sir Hugo Greymere

She smiled.

"Hey Ally, look at this!"

Alex was pointing at the huge book. The ripped page had been replaced. A new one had taken its place. It read –

Sir Hugo Greymere.
Defender of the innocent.
Slayer of Dragons.
He died a hero.

"And all is right with the world," said a voice.

The children looked behind them, seeing Henry Sampson. He was walking up behind them, his craggy old face breaking into a smile.

"Mr Sampson?" said Ally, confused.

Sampson walked up to the glass case and cast his eye over the book and the Family Tree. "It's been a long time coming. My family have waited centuries. I'd almost given up hope." He held out his hand for the children to shake. "Let me introduce myself. I'm Henry Sampson Greymere."

Ally thought her jaw would drop through the stone floor. "You're a .... A Greymere?"

He smiled again. "Indeed. I don't like to be Lord of the Manor. Not many people round here know who I am. And the one's that do keep it to themselves. Not even your Father knows."

"You knew didn't you?" Ally said. "You knew about… Hugo."

He nodded. "I knew. My family have been here for centuries. We've lived here. We've worked here. And we've waited. You see, we couldn't help him. He had to help himself." He leaned on the case. "There have been people who lived in that cottage who have claimed they heard crying. Some have even said they've seen a ghostly figure. And some have seen nothing at all."

He turned to Ally.

"It's taken a very special set of circumstances to get to this point, Ally. It's taken you. And your young friend here."

Alex smiled.

"Thank you," said Henry, as he began to walk away.

"Mr Sampson!" called Ally.

He stopped and turned back.

"Do you know if he's okay?" she said. "Hugo, I mean."

Sampson smiled. "He's where he belongs." He turned and walked down the corridor.

Alex approached her. He put his hand on her shoulder. "You okay?"

She smiled. "Oh yeah." She kissed him on the cheek.

At that moment, her Dad walked round the corner. "Hey kids!" he called. "How about some dinner? Come on."

The three of them walked down the corridor, bright sunlight shining through the windows and for all of them, a feeling of happiness.

And peace.

The End

Author's Note

I have a number of plays published online at lazybeescripts.co.uk in various genres, including comedy, drama and horror.

If you would like to know more, please email me at damianwoods011@gmail.com